WOLF'S MATE

A CRESCENT MOON STORY

Katie Reus

Cover art: Jaycee of Sweet 'N Spicy Designs
Author website: www.katiereus.com

Wolf's Mate/Katie Reus -- 1st ed.

ISBN-13: 9781635560404
ISBN-10: 1635560403

eISBN-13: 9781635560398

Praise for the novels of Katie Reus

"...a wild hot ride for readers. The story grabs you and doesn't let go."
—*New York Times* bestselling author, Cynthia Eden

"Has all the right ingredients: a hot couple, evil villains, and a killer action-filled plot. . . . [The] Moon Shifter series is what I call Grade-A entertainment!" —Joyfully Reviewed

"I could not put this book down. . . . Let me be clear that I am not saying that this was a good book *for* a paranormal genre; it was an excellent romance read, *period.*" —All About Romance

"Reus strikes just the right balance of steamy sexual tension and nail-biting action....This romantic thriller reliably hits every note that fans of the genre will expect." —*Publishers Weekly*

"Prepare yourself for the start of a great new series! . . . I'm excited about reading more about this great group of characters."
—Fresh Fiction

"Wow! This powerful, passionate hero sizzles with sheer deliciousness. I loved every sexy twist of this fun & exhilarating tale. Katie Reus delivers!" —Carolyn Crane, RITA award winning author

"A sexy, well-crafted paranormal romance that succeeds with smart characters and creative world building." —Kirkus Reviews

Erica laid her head against Hudson's chest as she trailed her fingers up his rock-hard abs—and over his plethora of tattoos. Everything about him was muscular and defined, which was common among shifters, wolf or otherwise. But the tattoos? He was the first shifter she'd met who had so many. Most of them were linked to his original Scottish clan or pack related things. Luckily none of them were for any past lovers. Something she would never be okay with.

She knew her time with him was coming to an end, and though she wanted to stall even longer, she shouldn't. Not if she wanted to keep her heart in one piece. Mostly. Because it was cracking already at the thought of leaving him. Of leaving Montana.

"Keep touching me like that and I'm going to be inside you in another ten seconds," he murmured, his voice all rough and raspy, sending shivers down her spine.

The man just had to open that sexy mouth and she was mush. "You say that like it's a bad thing." The truth was it didn't matter if she was touching him, he couldn't seem to keep his hands off her. Something she very much appreciated. Because she liked orgasms. A lot.

"Stay another couple days," he murmured.

It was on the tip of her tongue to say yes. She desperately wanted to. One month with him wasn't enough.

But he hadn't offered her anything. He'd simply asked her 'to stay in Montana'. And while he might not be alpha of the Kendrick pack, he was second-in-command and terribly alpha in nature. Shifters like him went for what they wanted. If he wanted to claim her, for her to stay permanently, he would have asked for that. Simple as that. Because the male was over two hundred years old. He was being honest, she could give him that. He'd never promised her anything and she'd taken exactly what he'd been offering—a lot of fun.

So she might want him—and genuinely want more than just sex—but she wasn't going to throw herself at him. Hell no. She was going to walk away with her pride intact and head back to her own pack. Even if it carved her up inside to do so. Because sometime during the last month she'd fallen for him. Hard. It would have been impossible not to. He'd opened up about his past, brought her breakfast in bed—woke her up with oral sex almost every other morning—and was simply the sweetest man she'd ever met.

"We've been over this." She gently nipped at his bare chest. Damn she was going to miss him. For more reasons than the hard body underneath her.

"You're not on a schedule." He was dangerously close to pouting, which under any other circumstance, would have made her giggle.

But she didn't feel like laughing now. Not when the ache in her chest had settled in deep and wasn't letting up anytime soon.

She pushed up on the bed to look into those startling blue eyes. His dark hair was a little longer than most of his packmates, curling around his ears. "I might not be on a hard schedule, but I still need to get back. It's been a year. My pack needs me." After college she'd started working at one of the pack's salons. Then when the owner had up and mated—and moved—Erica had decided to reevaluate her own life.

So she'd taken a year to herself and roamed around the globe, mainly sticking to the United States. During the last month of her trip, she'd been traveling across Montana and had met the very sexy Hudson Kendrick. She'd never imagined meeting someone like him on her trip. All sexy, surly and incredibly giving in the bedroom—soooo giving. And everything about him was real and honest. What you saw with Hudson, you got.

In response, he simply growled at her, but there was no heat behind it. Not that it mattered, her wolf side knew on an intrinsic level that he would never actually hurt her so even his most terrifying growl didn't scare her. He started to say something when his phone buzzed.

Cursing, he snatched it off the bedside table and then cursed again when he looked at the screen. "It's my brother, we're having another issue on the border. I've got to take care of this."

Though she hated to do so, she rolled off him and let him get up. It was hard not to admire the view as he picked up his discarded jeans from the floor and tugged them on, covering all of that sexy bronze skin.

"I'm probably just going to head out while you're gone," she said carefully, watching him for his reaction.

He froze for a moment before turning to glare at her. "At least wait until I can take you to the airport."

She wanted to say yes but gave a noncommittal grunt. His brother, the alpha, had offered to fly her back to her home in Alabama on his private jet anytime she wanted. Apparently, there was a pilot currently on standby. Which was really nice, but also bad because she'd kept extending her stay for the last week. Because Hudson kept pushing for 'one more day'. Erica knew that if she waited for him to take her to the airport, she'd give him another day, and then another.

And then that whole pride thing? Yeah, she wasn't so sure she'd walk away with it intact. She'd do something stupid and then getting over him would be even harder. Try, impossible.

When Hudson's phone buzzed again, he did that sexy growling thing as he looked at it. More colorful curses followed before he tugged a long-sleeved T-shirt over his head. She stayed in bed, just watching him move, all lethal efficiency. Once he was dressed, with his boots on, he stalked toward the bed and leaned over her, placing both hands on either side of her head, effectively caging her in. Then he crushed his mouth to hers, a possessive claiming she felt all the way to her core.

Unfortunately, he didn't seem to want to claim her in reality. Because sex wasn't enough to keep her here. She wanted more than that. Something she hadn't realized until she'd met Hudson. The sex was great—better than great—but she needed more.

"I'll see you soon. Be naked when I get back."

Oh no, not responding to that. Nope. Because she wouldn't be here when he got back.

Once he was gone, she gave it five minutes before packing up her small bag and trying to ignore the spreading ache in her chest. She had to do this now. She hadn't brought much with her on her trip, because it was a whole lot easier to travel light. Now she was grateful for that. The sharpest sense of melancholy filtered through her as she hefted her bag and backpack up. It was time to go home.

So why did it feel like she was making the biggest mistake of her life by leaving? And why did it feel like she was leaving home instead?

CHAPTER TWO

One month later

Erica stretched her legs out, digging her toes into the sand. The moon was high overhead, illuminating the ocean and shore in front of her. The sound of her packmates partying nearby was impossible to miss. Laughter, shouts to 'turn the music up' and other typical party revelry normally lifted her spirits.

Not tonight.

When the wind shifted slightly she scented her alpha—though she didn't hear Grant. He was so stealthy, she was pretty certain that it was second nature to him, that he wasn't trying to sneak up on her. It was simply part of who he was.

"Hey, little wolf," Grant said, settling next to her on the sand. His shoes were off too and he dug his feet into the sand next to her. "What are you doing out here by yourself?"

Meaning, why wasn't she enjoying the party like everyone else? Wolves loved to party more than most shifters. But she wasn't in a party mood.

She lifted a shoulder, inhaling the salty air. Normally it calmed her nerves, but lately nothing seemed to do that. "Just not feeling social."

He nudged her once with his shoulder. "Come on. What's really going on?"

Erica hadn't felt like herself since she'd returned home. She hadn't even taken on a permanent position in any of the pack's various business establishments. She'd been floating around, sometimes working at the casino, or the hotel, the Crescent Moon Bar, and she'd even temped at the new salon—her specialty was nails and waxing, something that she actually enjoyed. But even that hadn't brought her any sense of fulfilment. The pack that had raised her, this place she'd always considered home, for some reason didn't feel right anymore. And that depressed the hell out of her. She almost felt as if she was refusing to put down roots since returning home. Because she wasn't sure she wanted to stay put.

Clearing her throat, she tried to answer his question. "Everything's changed since I got back. Or I guess I should say everything changed while I was gone, which I expected." But she hadn't expected to almost feel like an outsider in her own pack. Everyone had been welcoming on her return but a couple of her friends had mated and moved on, literally. They'd joined other packs across the country. Her former place of employment was no longer open because the owner had moved to North Carolina and joined another pack. The new salon didn't feel like 'home' to her.

But the real reason she felt so out of sorts was because she'd left Hudson behind. He hadn't been too happy with her for splitting while he'd been off on that patrol thing.

Yeah, it had been pretty weak of her to leave like that but she'd told him she was going to. And her own sanity ranked above his annoyance. It wasn't as if she'd just cut him out of her life either. They'd been talking, Skyping and texting over the last month. A lot. The man called her every night no matter what. But… he hadn't said anything about wanting to mate.

Grant wrapped an arm around her shoulders and squeezed her close. "Does this have something to do with your stay at the Kendrick pack in Montana?"

She stiffened slightly. She hadn't told anyone about Hudson or her time there. It wasn't a secret or anything, but she hadn't felt like talking about the wolf. "Why do you ask?"

"Because you look how I felt when Talia wouldn't talk to me."

Erica had been younger then but she definitely remembered. Her alpha had mated with a wonderful human and Talia had made him work for it. Luckily for the entire pack it hadn't taken Grant too long to pull his head out of his ass either.

"Okay, fine, this is over a guy," she said.

He let his arms drop and wrapped them around his knees as he faced the ocean. The waves were quiet tonight, gently pushing against the shore in a soft rhythm. "Want to talk about it?"

"Not particularly." Not even with her alpha, a male she trusted more than anyone.

He made a sort of grunting sound. "That's fine but don't bottle it up for too long. It's not healthy. And if you need me to kick someone's ass, just say the word."

A startled laugh bubbled out of her at her alpha's slightly juvenile threat. "Thanks, but he's not a bad guy. He... asked me to stay." She wasn't going to tell Grant who Hudson was since he was the second in command and their two packs were allied. No need to cause any drama where it was unnecessary.

"Why didn't you stay?"

She lifted her shoulder again. "He didn't offer me anything but a good time."

Her alpha nodded slowly. "Sometimes men are dumbasses."

She giggled at that. "Yeah, so are women."

"Not responding to that," he muttered.

Laughing again, she nudged him with her shoulder once just as the scent of a dead fish wafted up from the shore.

It hit her so startlingly fast she wasn't prepared for the nausea that welled up. Without having time to jump up, she twisted to the left and away from Grant and tossed up the contents of her stomach. Which, unfortunately, was a lot.

As soon as she was done, she actually felt better, even if she was surprisingly weak. She was a shifter and couldn't remember the last time she'd been sick. What the heck had just happened?

Belatedly she realized that her alpha was rubbing her back in soft circles.

"Sorry about that," she rasped out, getting ready to push to her feet and get away from the mess.

"You're pregnant," he said as he jumped to his feet with the agility of a very old shifter. He held out a hand for her.

As she took his outstretched hand, she started to deny it but then realized, holy crap, she was... pregnant. Oh, she was so pregnant. And suddenly some things made a whole lot more sense. She'd been so caught up in her own issues that she hadn't even realized that there was another explanation to her mood swings and her strange nausea over the last week. Because hello, she was a wolf shifter. She did not get sick.

"Holy shit," she muttered.

Grant blinked once. "Are you just realizing it now?"

She simply nodded because she couldn't find any more words as they headed up the sand toward the pack-owned beach front condo complex. Oh no. No, no, no. How the heck could she be pregnant?

Scratch that, she knew *exactly* how it had happened. But... when she'd gone into heat they'd used condoms. So. Many. Condoms.

Now... she was pregnant.

Too many emotions seized her so that it was all she could do to breathe. This was not supposed to happen like this. And not with a man who clearly didn't want to mate with her.

And he'd asked her exactly twice to come back to Montana. But he still hadn't offered her anything, he hadn't asked her to mate him and she wasn't going to move away from her pack for anything less.

Not to mention he hadn't offered to come live here. She wouldn't ask it of him anyway, but the offer would be nice and would have assuaged her agitated wolf. Because right now her wolf side was anxious and edgy. Part of that was sexual frustration but more than that, she missed Hudson.

She'd been the one who'd told Hudson that they needed to see if the intensity of what they shared was real, if it wore off with distance. The intensity hadn't worn off for her.

And when they Skyped, it was worse because she could look into those clear blue eyes, and see exactly how much he missed her, and how much he *wanted* her. That lust wasn't enough for her, though. Because that shit did fade. It was just a matter of time. And it cut deep that the intense feelings, that bone deep mating hunger, seemed to be only one sided.

He was well over a century older than her, so she knew exactly what his generation was like. When they wanted something, they went after it. There really wasn't an in between.

So without offering her a mating, he'd made it clear that all he wanted was sex and fun from her.

And now… hell, now she needed to tell him she was pregnant. Only after she'd confirmed it for certain, of course, but her instinct was telling her that she was.

"You want me to call an out of town healer?" Grant asked quietly as they reached the gate that led to the condo's Olympic-sized pool.

She looked through the gate to see Grant's mate dancing, her long midnight-dark hair free as she laughed at something another packmate had said. Twinkle lights glittered over the pool and makeshift dance area. "Go be with your mate," she said, looking back at him. "I'm going to sneak around the side and head up to my condo through the front. I'll make a call in the morning. Oh…" She glanced back toward the beach where she'd left a lovely mess.

"I'll take care of it." He kissed her on the forehead before opening the gate.

Erica hurried away, down the side of the huge complex, using the wall that surrounded the pool area as a barrier between her and her packmates. She knew that some of them would ask about her absence and Grant, being the alpha he was, would easily deflect any questions.

None of that really mattered now. She did have some calls to make. First, to a nearby healer so she could get a checkup.

But first, she was going to brush her teeth. Because gross.

And soon she was going to have to tell Hudson that she was pregnant. And he was the father.

CHAPTER THREE

Hudson flew back through the air as his brother slammed a fist in the middle of his chest. The blow jarred him straight to his bones. Luckily, he was a shifter and over two hundred years old. He was hard to break. But he shouldn't have let his brother, alpha or not, get the drop on him so easily. They'd been sparring the last hour and that was some rookie shit right there.

Standing over him, a trace of disbelief on his face, Malcolm shook his head as he held out a hand. "Seriously, that was weak."

Cursing at himself, Hudson took the extended hand and jumped to his feet. "I know. I have no excuse." They'd come to the gym to get some extra training in—and Hudson had wanted to expend some of his pent-up energy. He was beyond sexually frustrated and practically climbing the fucking walls.

Malcolm lifted a shoulder. "A female is a good excuse, but you're right, *you* don't have an excuse. You let your woman go."

"I didn't let her go," he snarled. For the last month his brother had avoided talking about Erica, and Hudson was grateful for it.

His brother snorted. "You sure about that?"

He turned his back on Malcolm and strode toward the bench against one of the walls. Sometimes they sparred outside, but occasionally they sparred indoors on the mats. It was icy out today so they'd opted for the gym. He grabbed his water bottle and drank half of it as his brother strolled up next to him and grabbed another water bottle.

"I don't get you, brother. I know how you feel about her, and if it was me—"

"It's not you." He slammed his bottle down on the bench. "She's younger than us, she's from a different generation. I don't want to push her too hard too fast."

"She's not that young. Even if she is from a different generation, she's not a different species. To any outsider, it just looks like you let her go. So what do you think that looks like to her?"

He ground his molars, resisting the urge to punch his brother. Talking about Erica wasn't on the agenda today. His wolf was too edgy. "She wanted space. She said she wanted to see if the intensity between us wore off once we had distance." He rolled his shoulders but it did nothing to ease the tension hammering away at him. As far as intensity, nothing had worn off. He'd known it wouldn't. The whole separation thing was bullshit. He'd wanted to tie her to his bed and keep her there. But that was fucking psychotic so he'd let his female go. Barely.

He felt as if he could crawl out of his skin right now. Hell, he felt like that all day every day. All he wanted to do was shift to his wolf and run and run until maybe he tired himself out and got some sort of relief from all the raging insanity racing through him seemingly twenty-four-seven. All he could do was think about her. AKA, obsess about her. She was in his head, in his damn bones—an addiction he never wanted to get over.

Malcolm simply grunted as he set his own bottle down. "So do you want to go another round and bring your A game, or are you ready to call it a day?"

"I'm ready to go."

His brother's mouth curved up into a smirk that Hudson knew well. Right now, Malcolm was looking for a fight. He could sense it.

"You sure, little brother?"

Yep, when Malcolm started calling him that, Hudson knew. Malcolm wasn't in alpha mode right now, but he *was* in big brother mode. Which meant he was in jackass mode.

"Don't start with me." Because Hudson was not feeling it today. He'd requested solitary patrols because he didn't want to bite the heads off any pups simply because he was in a perpetually bad mood.

"I don't blame you for being down on yourself. If I couldn't hold on to my female, I'd be feeling pretty shitty too."

Hudson growled low in his throat as he strode onto the mats. "You're not going to bait me."

His brother simply stepped out onto the mat, a gleam in his blue eyes. "Seems to me that I'm just stating a fact. You offered to mate with Erica and she left you."

"I didn't ask her to mate," Hudson snapped out. He hadn't wanted to push her too fast and have her run from him. He'd thought he was making the right choice, taking things slow.

"I knew it! No wonder she left your dumb ass." Malcolm rushed at him like a linebacker.

Hudson was ready for him this time, however. When they sparred like this, it was in human form only, no claws or canines.

As they rolled to the floor he got in a solid blow to Malcolm's jaw but his brother went with it, rolling them over and landing an elbow across Hudson's face.

He savored the bite of pain, needing to feel something other than the emotional bullshit he'd been dealing with. Because he couldn't shrug it off, couldn't get rid of it, couldn't do *anything* about it. Not until Erica was back— not until he brought her back.

They rolled around like pups for a solid ten minutes, punching and snarling until finally Hudson slammed his hand against the mat. "I'm done," he rasped out.

Laughing lightly, his brother collapsed next to him on the mat and stretched out. "What the hell, Hudson? Why didn't you ask her to mate with you? I know how you feel about her. Everyone in the pack does."

Hudson lay on his back as well, staring up at the ceiling. "I didn't want to scare her off. But I did ask her to stay, multiple times. And I've asked her to come back. Multiple times." They'd even had phone sex a couple times but during the last week, he'd felt her pulling away from him. And he knew it was his fault. He thought he'd been right in going slow with her. This younger generation of wolves was different than his. He'd known that he couldn't go all barbarian on her and tell her that she was his. Yeah, that would've gone over really well. She'd have cut him out of her life.

"You offered her nothing," Malcolm said quietly, the barest hint of disappointment in his words. That got Hudson more than anything. "Don't get me wrong, you were good to her and I know how you feel about her, but I don't know that she does. And if you want to keep a female like that, you need to step up your game. Spell it out."

"What the hell do you know about game, old man?" His brother was only ten years older.

Malcolm jumped to his feet after landing one last elbow to the ribs and dodging out of the way. "I know that a sweet female like that certainly isn't going to wait around for you. She'll move on, find someone new. I guarantee someone in her pack is going to be the shoulder she cries on when it becomes clear that you aren't man enough to claim her—"

Hudson's canines and claws extended as the very real urge to attack his brother surged through him.

Laughing his ass off, Malcolm ran from the room acting nothing like the true alpha he was, and exactly like a big brother.

Something Hudson needed right now.

Taking a deep breath, he got his wolf under control. Though he hated to admit it, his brother was right. He should have just gone all wolf and made it clear she was his. He'd actually already booked a last-minute flight with their pilot. He was going to see Erica tonight. He couldn't be away from her any longer. His wolf couldn't stand it. Neither could he.

He felt as if he was hanging on by a thread being separated from her. Maybe he would screw things up by going all caveman on her but he would never know unless he tried. He'd been trying to act like someone he wasn't and he'd lost the woman he loved.

He couldn't deny the wolf he was anymore. It was time to make things right and claim the female he should have made his weeks ago.

CHAPTER FOUR

Erica couldn't contain the butterflies in her stomach as the pilot finally shut off the engine. They'd been sitting on the tarmac inside the Kendrick pack's territory for a few minutes as he did whatever it was he was supposed to do. That was definitely one of the nice things about being part of a successful pack. Having a private plane at your disposal. More or less anyway. Wolves in general preferred to fly solo or with their packmates only.

Airports tended to make her wolf edgy. Being surrounded by so many humans, so much noise and the cacophony of scents. It was unlikely that anything would set her wolf off but that fear was always there, that something could startle her wolf and she might change in the middle of a crowded airport.

As she waited for the pilot to emerge from the cockpit she tried calling Hudson again but his phone still went to voicemail. She hadn't talked to him in about twelve hours. Which... wasn't abnormal. But once she'd confirmed this morning that yes, she was pregnant, she'd made plans to return to Montana as soon as she could. When Hudson hadn't answered his phone, she'd decided to bite the bullet and call Malcolm instead.

25

When she'd told him that she was coming back for a few days the alpha had seemed inordinately pleased about it. He'd told her that Hudson was on a special patrol. He'd been kind of cryptic about it actually. Alphas could be secretive sometimes. Still, she'd tried to call Hudson multiple times before she'd gotten on the plane and now… It wasn't like him to keep his phone off so he must've had to go dark for some kind of mission.

That might be why Malcolm hadn't explained to her what his brother was doing. She wasn't part of their pack so she wasn't privy to any sensitive information.

No, she was just a girl who'd spent a month with Hudson. Ugh.

The pilot, one of her packmates, stepped out of the cockpit and smiled at her. "How's your stomach feeling?"

She'd told Julian that she was pregnant just to give him a heads up if she got sick. "Surprisingly good." Saltine crackers of all things seemed to be working. And the healer she'd seen this morning had given her something for this flight. All-natural and created specifically for wolf shifters. Because remedies that worked for humans didn't always work for her kind.

"Good. If you're ready then, I just got a call. Malcolm is here to greet you."

She blinked once as she stood and picked up her purse. "Do you mean Hudson?"

"No, the alpha is here." At that, Julian opened the door and let the built-in stairs down. "I'll grab your bag, so just head on down."

She certainly hadn't expected Malcolm to meet her. And she wasn't sure what to make of it. She wasn't another alpha or high up enough in the hierarchy to warrant the alpha of another pack actually meeting her at the airport. She also couldn't quell the disappointment that it wasn't Hudson meeting her.

She'd thought about telling him that she was pregnant over Skype, but this was the kind of thing she needed to do in person. They had a lot to talk about, logistics to figure out... stuff she didn't even remotely want to think about but knew that they had to. Luckily, they had a few months yet to make any big decisions but he had a right to know. Even if she was scared about how he'd react. He'd once made a comment about not even wanting pups. So maybe... ugh. Not going there now.

Her own parents had died when she was young and she wanted to make sure that both she and Hudson were involved in their pups' lives. Yep, pups. They were having twins.

She'd barely wrapped her mind around the fact that she was going to be a parent, let alone to two pups. But the healer had been certain of it.

She realized that Julian had said something to her so she smiled, mumbled something and headed for the opening. Erica barely remembered descending the stairs or greeting Malcolm but when she found herself in the passenger seat of an SUV she realized that Hudson spent time in this vehicle because it smelled like him.

Like the forest, all earthy and dark.

She inhaled deeply as Malcolm put her bag in the back and once he finally slid into the front seat she felt somewhat back to normal.

"How was the flight," he asked as he strapped in. "You need anything on the way back to the compound?"

The 'compound' was a huge spread of property in a densely forested area with a lot of cabins spread out where the pack all lived. "Flight was good and nope, I'm good. I'm surprised you met me here."

He gave her a small smile. "I wouldn't be a very good alpha if I didn't meet..." He cleared his throat as he trailed off. "Listen, I've got something to tell you. When you called me, Hudson was already on his way to Alabama to see you."

"Wait... what?" She could have just waited for him then, something Malcolm clearly knew. What the alpha didn't know was that she could have gotten this weight off her chest a lot sooner. It was weighing on her and she desperately wanted to tell Hudson.

"Yeah and I didn't tell you because I wanted *you* back here. And I wanted *him* to sweat it out, to work for this a little."

"Work for... what exactly?" Because if Hudson had wanted her, he could have had her. All he'd had to do was ask her for more.

He just gave her a sideways look before focusing on the road again. It was dark out, with a smattering of stars overhead, but the cloud cover was hazy enough that there wasn't much illumination. "So are you back for a while, or...?"

"Ah..." She felt weird telling the actual alpha that she wasn't sure yet. "I don't really know. A week at least. I just need to talk to Hudson about some stuff."

"What stuff?"

"You're nosy." The words were out before she could stop herself. She blinked once. "I'm sorry, that was rude."

He just laughed. "I am nosy. Like every wolf in my pack... but I won't push. And just so we're clear, if you do want to join my pack, you're more than welcome."

She blinked again. "Thank you." That was a generous offer, especially since he hadn't added a disclaimer about her being with Hudson or... anything. And an alpha wouldn't make a mistake like that. When she'd first met him, she'd been surprised that Malcolm was actually an alpha. She could sense his power and knew how old he was, but he was so laid back about things. Unlike her own alpha, who could be intense and scary when he wanted. Intellectually she knew that Malcolm was probably all those things too, but she'd only seen his softer side.

"You'd be a good addition to our pack—not that I'm trying to poach you. But I did let Grant know you're welcome to transfer if you so choose. I don't want you to be blindsided if he says something."

That was a whole lot to take in. "Thank you again. I... still can't believe you didn't tell Hudson I was headed this way." She didn't care if she was pushing the issue, it surprised her and she wasn't sure she understood the alpha's reasoning. Because it seemed a little mean.

The grin he gave her was nothing short of mischievous. "My brother can be pigheaded sometimes. Trust me, he deserves this."

Erica just shook her head but settled back against the leather seat and enjoyed being in the warm vehicle. Maybe this little reprieve from having to tell Hudson wasn't such a bad thing. She could figure out the exact right way to tell him because right now, she had nothing good other than 'Surprise, I'm pregnant. With twins'.

Ugh.

* * *

Hudson's lush, spicy scent teased Erica before she'd even opened her eyes. Pushing up in bed, she wasn't exactly surprised to see him standing in the doorway of the guest bedroom. But her heart skipped a beat just the same.

"How long have you been standing there?" she murmured, unsure what time it was and not particularly caring.

He let out a sexy growl as he raked a hand through his still too-long hair. "You don't want to know."

"If you were human that would be kinda weird… and maybe it is weird for shifters too." But she didn't care at all. "When did you get back? And… what time is it?"

He strode into the room and stripped off his sweater as he approached the bed. "It's five in the morning and I just got back. Gonna kick my brother's ass later," he muttered.

"Did I say you could join me?" She kept her expression neutral as he reached the edge of the king-sized bed.

He paused in surprise and she didn't bother to fight her smile. "You can join me—but no sex." She was too tired—though for him, she'd make an exception. But not tonight. Or this morning as it were. No, she wanted to tell him why she was really here before anything happened between them. If it did at all.

His expression relaxing, he slid into the bed, as if crawling in next to her was the most natural thing in the world. "I'm glad you're here," he murmured as he brushed his lips over hers. "Though I'm sad you're wearing clothing." He pulled her close to him as he settled against the pillow.

Tired as she was, she snuggled right up on him, laying her head on his chest. It was a relief to have his arms around her, as if she'd been missing something and hadn't even realized it until he was holding her again. She wanted to tell him why she was really here, the words were on the tip of her tongue. But what would a couple hours change? She wanted to enjoy this reunion in case things didn't go well when she broke the news.

"I can't believe your brother let you fly all the way to the gulf coast." Though she was pleased he'd made the effort to go see her. "Any particular reason you decided to go there without calling me first?"

"Yeah. Decided to bring you back here."

She lifted her head at his brusque tone. "What?" She couldn't tell if he was being serious or not.

He shrugged, a dark glint in his gaze she'd never seen before. Even without any lights on, there was enough outside illumination to see the harsh lines of his face. "We'll talk in a while. I need sleep too."

She wanted to push harder, but exhaustion pulled her under, making her lethargic and telling her to take advantage and get some damn sleep. She'd heard other shifters talk about what it was like to be pregnant and it was no joke.

Sleep was everything right now. Well, sleep and the very sexy man she'd wrapped herself around. She couldn't believe he'd come straight back from her hometown after reaching his destination. And given the time, he would have had to.

What did 'bring her back here' even mean? Because it wasn't an offer to mate. And she wasn't going to drive herself crazy trying to figure him out either. Not now anyway.

No, she was going to get some rest and prep for his reaction—of which she was almost a hundred percent certain was going to be awful. He'd made it clear he didn't want pups, had never planned for them in his life. Now... well, too damn bad. It was happening whether he wanted it or not. And if he didn't want to be involved in their lives, then she'd deal with that if the time came.

"Hey," he murmured, squeezing her slightly. "You just went all tense. What's wrong?"

"Nothing." She didn't raise her head to meet his gaze, just remained where she was, listening to his steady heartbeat.

She was surprised when he didn't push but grateful as she closed her eyes. Forcing all thoughts of later out of her mind, she let sleep take over.

CHAPTER FIVE

Hudson watched Erica across the kitchen table of the guest cabin. She'd stayed in here a few nights during that first month when she'd come to the compound. But once they'd started sleeping together she'd spent all of her nights in his cabin.

Where she belonged.

He'd missed her so much this past month, and seeing her in person, holding her for the past few hours in bed had only solidified what he'd already known.

He never should have let her go in the first place. He was going to remedy that mistake right now. "You sure you don't want coffee?"

She paused and nodded. "Herbal tea sounds better this morning."

He stood to start making her tea, knowing she had a stash here. He hadn't changed anything since she'd left. "I saw your bag. It's not big," he said carefully, even as he wondered why the hell it wasn't bigger. Filled with all of her things. Because she should be staying. "If you're moving here, we can easily get everything shipped here."

She blinked in surprise and he realized he'd been right. She wasn't back for good. He hadn't wanted to ask her when he'd slipped into bed with her. Not when he'd simply wanted to enjoy holding her.

"I… don't know what my plans are yet." She cleared her throat. "However, I'm impressed you flew out to see me." Her tone was slightly tart, surprising him. "I didn't think you ever left your pack's land."

He frowned at her words and the underlying annoyance in her tone. Before he could respond a sharp knock on the cabin door made both of them turn. He could see through the window on the kitchen door that it was Ursula, one of the sentries currently on duty patrolling their land. "Come in," he called out.

Ursula stepped inside wearing her standard cargo pants and long-sleeved sweater. She smiled brightly when she saw Erica. "Hey girl, we missed you."

"I've missed you too." She stood and hugged the other woman tightly. Erica was about half a head shorter than Ursula, who always had her white-blonde hair in a braid down her back.

"You better stay this time. And I definitely need you to do something about this," she pointed to her head, indicating her hair.

Hudson wasn't sure what his packmate was talking about. Her hair was pulled back into a tight braid and looked exactly like it always did.

But Erica had charmed all of his packmates with free hairstyles and nail stuff. And she was talented. She'd gone to college to get a business degree—at her alpha's urging—but she'd also gone to cosmetology school. She'd once told him that she loved making people feel better about themselves.

Erica smiled. "I'll definitely set aside some time for you while I'm here."

"Good, but even if you can't find the time, it's okay. And we're definitely having a party for you tonight," Ursula said, grinning.

Erica looked surprised by this and then looked at him for confirmation. He simply nodded because the party had been his idea. Not that he needed to take credit for it.

"Look, I hate to interrupt you guys," Ursula said, clearing her throat. "Especially since you just got here, but a couple of our wolves got into it with a group from the Lincoln pack. All teenagers and mostly harmless. But with everything going on lately along the border, I figured this was something you and Malcolm should both take care of. He's out for his morning run now, so there's no way to get a hold of him."

Hudson simply nodded, inwardly cursing at the interruption. He and Erica hadn't been awake for very long and all he wanted to do was spend time with her, to tell her that he wanted her for a mate if she'd have him. But there were some things that he had to take care of. Especially something like this. And he wasn't going to open up to Erica with an audience.

"Meet me by the west gate in five minutes."

Once she was gone, he turned to Erica. "I'm sorry—"

"You don't have to apologize, trust me, I definitely understand."

He knew she did. There was no annoyance or recrimination in her expression. He still wanted to know why she'd traveled all this way to see him, because he knew she had a reason other than just wanting to see him. Something that depressed the hell out of him. "As soon as I get back I'll move your stuff into my cabin." Her eyes widened slightly, as if she was surprised by his words, but it was time for him to step up and be the wolf that he really was. To claim his female. "I'm going to grab a quick cup of coffee and head out. If you need anything, I'll leave a list of phone numbers for available packmates."

"I've got a bunch of numbers saved in my phone already," she said softly. "I'll be fine, trust me. Probably get roped into doing manicures." She wiggled her own fingers, which were painted with pink and gold chevrons.

Crossing the distance to her, he bent down and brushed his lips over hers, resisting the urge to deepen the kiss. If he did, he knew himself well enough that he'd be sorely tempted to blow off his duties. Something he'd never done before, not in hundreds of years.

But Erica brought out a new side to him. And it was past time that he accepted it, hell, embraced it.

CHAPTER SIX

"When you move here, you should open your own salon. I guarantee we'd keep you in business. And so will Alex's pack... if things with them ever smooth out," Chelsea added on, rolling her eyes.

For the last couple hours Erica had been hanging out with a handful of Hudson's packmates, and now it was just down to her and Chelsea, a tough warrior who'd taken Erica under her wing pretty much the first day she'd arrived on Kendrick land. She cleared her throat, not sure how to respond to the 'when you move here' bit. She wasn't sure if she *was* going to move here. She wasn't sure of anything. Somehow, she still found herself saying, "Where would I open up shop? Is there office space in town?" Because if she did start her own business, she wanted a separation from the actual pack land. It would be easier to expand her business that way.

Not that she was even thinking of doing that... was she?

"There are a couple office buildings in a strip mall that the pack owns. And if you decide to join the pack, *hint hint,* you'll be able to use it, no problem. One of the open spaces is next to a coffee shop, also pack owned. You'd get extra foot traffic from that alone.

It definitely gave her something to think about. "I'll think about it," she murmured, not remotely ready to commit to anything.

"I don't know what there is to think about now that you've found your mate."

She simply looked up from painting an intricate wolf paw on one of Chelsea's nails and raised an eyebrow. "Seriously? Would you just drop everything and move to a new state for a guy?"

"First, I'd never move for a man. For the right woman, probably. And I would totally move to another state if my new mate's pack was as awesome as ours is." She grinned widely as she added, "I do understand though. Moving is such a huge thing. Besides, who says he won't move back home with you?"

Hmm. Erica paused at that, then went back to painting another nail. She was going to add some little sparkles to Chelsea's pinkies when the female wasn't looking. "So say I was going to stay. Do you think I could look at that office space this week?" She didn't want to just sit around waiting for Hudson to finish his pack business. She understood that he was second-in-command and was naturally going to be busy. Before her year of travel, she'd been busy pretty much every second of the day too. Kinda like most wolves. They had so much damn energy it was almost a given.

"As soon as you finish these wicked looking nails, I'll drive you myself." Chelsea smiled as Erica put the finishing touch on her pinky. She frowned once at the little jewel then shrugged.

"It won't take long to dry," Erica said, putting the cap on the adhesive.

"Perfect. Once we've checked out the space and you see how awesome it is, I'm taking you to lunch. As a thank you for this," she wiggled her sparkly fingers. "Plus, it's going to drive Hudson crazy when he finds out where I took you."

"Why would it drive him crazy that you're taking me to lunch?" It wasn't as if Chelsea was interested in Erica romantically.

"No, he's going to be annoyed *where* I took you. There's a pretty boy wolf who isn't part of our pack that runs a restaurant in our territory. He's cool with the pack, but just trust me, it will totally drive Hudson nuts. The straight females in our pack go crazy over this guy. And Hudson is in that frenzied stage where he wants to claim his mate. He's gonna get mad just on principle."

Erica didn't know about all that but she wasn't going to comment on Hudson's 'frenzied' state—since Chelsea was wrong. "I didn't realize you liked poking at your packmates. I'm making a mental note of that."

Chelsea giggled. "I would never poke you. I just like to mess with the males. Half the time they seem to have their heads up their asses. They kind of deserve it."

Erica didn't fight the laugh that bubbled up. Chelsea reminded her a little bit of her packmate Sarah. It sent a bittersweet spread of warmth through her chest as she thought about her pack. She missed them, but she was starting to realize she could definitely settle in here. Who was she kidding, she could settle in here even if she hadn't gotten to know so many of Hudson's packmates. Because Hudson was here.

Annoyingly sexy Hudson.

About half an hour later, Erica stepped into the empty office space with Chelsea who kept jingling the keys in her hand. It was chilly inside, probably because no one had thought to set the heat very high since the space wasn't in use.

"Please put those in your pocket, you're driving me crazy," Erica said as she scanned the space.

"Ha, sorry." The jingling thankfully stopped.

Erica eyed the big open room with interest. It was seriously plain and boring. Which wasn't exactly a bad thing. She could paint it a soft robin's egg blue and mix it with gray undertones. They could add on a private room to do waxing and potentially massages. She'd have to hire some humans likely, especially if there weren't any wolves with experience or the right training around.

"I can literally see the wheels in your head turning."

Laughing lightly, she glanced over at Chelsea who was watching her curiously.

"I'm just thinking about everything I can do to this place. It will be really easy to set this up as a salon as long as there's no issue with the plumbing." It'd certainly be expensive though, at least to start it up. New chairs, sinks… there was a lot to think about. Luckily, she'd majored in business and was a math nerd. Numbers were her thing so she'd have to start figuring things out.

"I knew bringing you here was a good idea."

Nodding slowly, she turned back to the giant room and started to feel seriously excited. It might not work out but the thought of running her own salon… Yeah that was something she could get on board with. She'd worked with her former packmate for only a few months before Charlie had closed up shop and moved with her own mate to his territory. Now, Erica wanted something for herself. Something that was hers. And she needed to embrace this huge new adventure. Moving was scary but it didn't have to be such a terrifying thought.

Not if she had something that was hers so she felt like a contributing member of the pack. And she would have Hudson. Deep down she knew that. Even if they never got mated, even if they just co-parented and had some sort of relationship… The thought of that made her feel blah inside so she shoved it away.

One step at a time. For all she knew, he was going to be angry at the news and send her packing. She wasn't certain she believed that, but she had to be ready for the possibility.

CHAPTER SEVEN

"I'm getting sick of this shit," Malcolm growled.

Hudson nodded as they both headed across the hard, cold earth toward the outdoor party being held for Erica. "I'm frustrated with Alex's pack too. And there's a reason you're alpha and I'm not." Because Hudson would have crossed territory boundaries and started kicking ass after today's bullshit. Which was not a diplomatic way to handle anything. Especially with Alex's pack. They'd been neighbors and friendly enough for decades. And they went back even further with Alex—about a century. He was a good alpha. "Something's got to be going on with him."

Malcolm nodded, his expression serious. "I've talked to him a few times. He's... distracted by something. I don't want to ruin our relationship but something's got to be done. I'm just not sure what it is yet."

Hudson nodded because he agreed with his brother. Today's little skirmish between the younger wolves had been a fairly normal occurrence. Two sets of teenagers, their own, and a handful from the neighboring pack got into a scuffle near their border. Both sets of wolves had been trying to assert their dominance. Nothing weird about that. But there had been far too many instances of vandalism—stolen property and property damage—

along their territory line in the last month. And *that* was not normal.

"If Alex can't keep his pack in check…" Hudson lifted a shoulder.

Malcolm nodded once, his expression grim. "Yeah, that's what I've been thinking too. There might be some dominance issues going on with his pack right now. It's hard to imagine anyone strong enough to challenge him, however. At least within his own pack."

Hudson nodded. Alex's pack had a strong core group just as the Kendrick pack did. The other alpha had a good second in command and strong warriors. Not only that, they also had a good balance of beta wolves. Something had to be screwing up the dynamic over there.

All thoughts of pack issues faded away as they reached the edge of the party. He immediately spotted Erica, talking to one of his pretty boy packmates, Jared. Her long, dark hair was braided, draped over one shoulder, right across one breast. God, he'd been fantasizing about those breasts for too damn long.

He could see little sparkles in her hair, under the moonlight and party lights. Probably the little stick-on stars she liked to use. He'd gotten them stuck to his hands and even found one on his cock after a particularly wild session with her.

In snug jeans definitely designed to drive him crazy and a wraparound sweater that showed off all sorts of cleavage, the wolf standing in front of her would have to be blind not to notice how incredible she was. And he didn't like the thought of any other male looking at her. Which he knew was unrealistic and stupid. His wolf simply didn't give a fuck.

"Try not to kill him," his brother murmured, no humor in his voice. "He's just talking to her. I'm going to call Alex, see if I can make contact and set up a meeting. This shit is going to end this week. I'm tired of it."

Hudson nodded, tuning out anything and everything as he stalked toward Erica and the male she was talking to. He ordered his wolf to *not* act like a jackass. She didn't seem to be aware of him as she laughed at something Jared said. In that moment he remembered the first time he'd seen her, spoken to her. It had only taken a couple days and he'd known that she was the one. He'd fallen hard and fast. That was the way with wolves. At least the males. They weren't like humans in that regard. When they met their mates, for the most part, they simply knew. But she didn't seem to have fallen as hard as he had. Yeah, she wanted him, there was no denying that. The sexual chemistry they had was off the charts. But he'd asked her to stay and she'd still left. It cut deep. He wondered how he would live like that if things were so one-sided.

He tried not to think about that first meeting, but the memory wouldn't leave him alone.

***

Two months ago

Hudson pulled up to the curb of the public airport a few feet back from the only person waiting, her suitcase sitting next to her as she typed something into her cell phone. He was running half an hour late and was annoyed that he was pulling babysitting duty because no one else was available. Okay, he just hadn't slept in forty-eight hours and was cranky in general.

But as he stared at the sexy shifter looking down at her phone, all annoyance faded. Wearing knee-high leather boots with what had to be four-inch heels over a pair of tight jeans and a formfitting sweater, he seriously hoped this was the she-wolf he was picking up.

She chose that moment to drop her phone into her purse and glance over at his SUV. The windows were tinted so there was no way she could see inside.

Realizing he was staring like a dumbass, he jumped out of the vehicle and rounded the front of it to greet her. Yep, she was definitely a shifter. Not human. Her scent gave her away immediately. And he liked what he smelled. "I'm Hudson, are you Erica?"

She smiled brightly. "Yes, thank you so much for picking me up. There's no way to get any transportation out here."

He snorted. This far out they were lucky they even had a public airport nearby. His pack almost never used it, not when they had a private plane and utilized the private airport near their land. *"I'm sorry you had to wait."* Before he'd been annoyed by this day trip, but now he actually did feel bad she'd had to wait so long.

She shrugged. *"No big deal. I appreciate your pack letting me visit this area."*

"Unless you're too tired, I can give you a tour of our land. We can take the four wheelers out or go for a long run."

She blinked once even as she smiled. *"Aren't you the second-in-command?"*

He nodded once.

She blinked again. *"Ah... if you're sure you're not too busy, that would be great. But honestly, I'm fine on my own. I've been trekking across the entire country and I don't mind exploring by myself."*

"I'll show you some of the best spots for running and hiking," he found himself saying. What the hell was wrong with him? He had shit to do, responsibilities, duties... he shouldn't be offering up any of his time. It had simply been too long since he'd had sex. That was all. He didn't know this woman and he certainly wasn't going to get involved with her. He was too damn busy anyway.

His wolf swiped at him, telling him he was very much wrong on that front. He ignored his dual nature and stepped closer to her, inhaling her peaches and sunshine scent. When he went to pick up her suitcase, she waved him away. But he grabbed the handle anyway. He knew that she was capable—she was a shifter after all and a wolf at that—but some intrinsic part of him wanted to do this.

After stowing it away in the back, he found her already sitting in the passenger seat so he got in the driver's side. "So how long have you been roaming?"

"Almost a year. This should be one of my last stops. I was thinking of heading down to Arizona after this but I'm not sure if I'll have time. I miss my pack."

"It's a lot of wide-open spaces here, your wolf should like it."

She smiled, and once again, he felt the intensity of her smile like a kick to his solar plexus. She was young, maybe thirty years old. It was impossible to pinpoint an exact age with wolves because physically she looked to be similar in age, but her level of power was exponentially less than his.

"Before we go exploring, would you mind stopping by Alma's Bed and Breakfast? I need to drop off my stuff and I want to get checked in."

He didn't like the idea as her staying there even if it was pack owned. For some reason he wanted her close to him. Okay maybe not just some reason, the woman was stunning and his wolf was drawn to her on a primal level. "We've got an empty cabin right now on pack land, why don't you just stay there? We own the bed and breakfast so it won't be a big deal to cancel your reservation. I can take care of it for you."

Surprise rolled off her. "I really don't want to impose on you guys. It's already nice enough that your alpha is allowing me on your territory."

"It's not an imposition, trust me. We've got thousands of acres. You won't be in anyone's way." And if the guest cabin happened to be close to his home, all the better. He wasn't going

to analyze why he was so desperate to have her on his pack's land.

"Well if you're sure it doesn't matter or I won't put anyone out, then that's great. I've been feeling a little cooped up the last couple days and need to run free for a while."

He could imagine, especially since she'd flown in on a regular plane. He knew that her own pack had a private jet but since she was roaming, she would've made her own travel accommodations. Now he wished his pack had offered to send their own jet to pick her up from her last stop. "When you head home, if your alpha doesn't send his jet, you can use our private plane."

"Ah... thanks." She blushed, making her even more adorable. Damn, she was definitely too young for him. But that did not matter to his wolf. And it didn't matter to him. Not right now when he was sitting in the enclosed cabin of his SUV and she smelled like heaven. The peaches and sunshine scent was damn near addicting and all he could think about was what it would be like to have her dig those heeled boots into his back as he ate her out.

Fuck. He blinked once and focused on the road. He did not need to get turned on right now and scare her off. No, he needed to act like a civilized wolf and not a caveman. He was too damn busy for a relationship or... whatever, anyway. He needed to get over whatever this was. Now.

CHAPTER EIGHT

Rolling his shoulders, Hudson managed to shove the memory from two months ago, far down. Right now, he needed to work on convincing his mate to stay permanently. To become part of his pack. To become his forever. He needed to stay in the present.

When he was about twenty feet away from her, she looked over and smiled when she spotted him. Then a trace of something he couldn't quite define flickered in her pretty eyes.

He'd sensed discomfort rolling off her this morning. Something was definitely wrong. He wanted to think that she'd come back because she'd decided to stay, that she couldn't live without him, but he had to face reality. She was definitely worried about something. It unsettled him.

As he approached, his packmate held out a hand. "Hey, Hudson—"

"Get lost," he snarled. So much for not being an asshole.

Erica's eyes widened but Jared just laughed as he muttered something about crazy wolves.

Erica stared at him for a long moment as the other male left. "That was incredibly rude."

He lifted a shoulder and clasped one of her hips in his hands, knowing full well the move was possessive. Tonight, he was walking a wire's edge of control. "He was standing too close to you."

Her gaze narrowed slightly. "Are you... jealous?" There was a hint of disbelief in her voice.

Why was she so surprised? "Call it whatever you want. I don't like any of my packmates getting too close to you. I only want my scent on you."

She shook her head as her lips curved up ever so slightly. "That shouldn't be quite so hot. Especially since it's completely barbaric."

"Maybe I'm not as civilized as you think," he murmured, lowering his head and giving her plenty of time to pull away if she wanted.

Instead she leaned up on tiptoe and met him half way.

Every part of him settled at the feel of her lips against his, her tight body pressed to his and though he wanted to deepen the kiss, to hoist her up so that she wrapped her legs around his waist—and find the nearest private spot in the nearby trees, it was clear they needed to talk about whatever was on her mind. And he wanted to make it clear that he wasn't letting her go.

Somehow, he pulled back. "Have you eaten anything yet?" He was going to steal her away from the party so they could talk and he needed to make sure that his woman was fed first. That was wolf-courting behavior 101. He had to take care of her.

"I… could actually eat a little bit more." She seemed surprised by that and he wasn't sure why.

"All right, I know what you like. I'll be right back."

She nodded, that bit of apprehension back in her gaze. It quickly dissipated as Ursula strode up to her, a smile on her face.

"Thank you again for the manicure. These tiny wolf paws you painted are sick…"

He tuned out the words of his packmate as he headed toward the food table, which was loaded down with a ridiculous amount of meats, cheeses and a little fruit. But mainly meat. Because wolves didn't eat much else.

By the time Hudson got a plate of food and a mixed drink for Erica, she was by herself again and watching some of his packmates dance to the music blasting from the DJ. He handed her a plate and felt ridiculously pleased when she smiled in appreciation. Making her happy could easily become his favorite pastime. Even if it did make him feel vulnerable to put himself out there.

"I grabbed a little bit of everything," he said, handing her a drink.

"Thanks. I'm starving tonight." She took a sip of the rum and Coke then froze.

To his surprise, she spit it out on the ground.

Alarm punched through him. "What's wrong?" He'd scented everything, as he did out of habit, and the drink had smelled fine.

She let out a strained laugh. "The Coke tastes flat."

He took it from her and took a sip but it tasted fine. Still, he set it on a nearby table. "Want me to get you something else to drink?"

She shook her head. "Nah. I'm okay. More hungry than anything."

Okay then. His woman had food. It was time to get down to business. "So, you're back and clearly there's something you want to talk to me about. Want to find some privacy?" He nodded toward the cluster of trees where some benches and tables were set up for extra seating. No one would bother them over there, not when the party was going so strong. And if someone did approach them, he would just wave them off.

She nodded, that tense expression returning.

He wanted to reach up and cup her face, to rub his thumbs over her soft skin and wipe away all traces of it. Panic bloomed inside him as he tried to think of what could be bothering her so badly. Her returning to Montana was supposed to be a good thing.

"I heard the party was your idea," she said quietly as they reached one of the farthest tables. The music and laughter faded somewhat.

He nodded as they sat. When he'd been in Gulf Shores—and his brother had called to tell him Erica was here—he'd called a few packmates and asked them to set something up. It wasn't as if wolves needed a reason to have a good time so getting this thing together so quickly had been easy. Hell, they usually just left the party lights strung up in the spring and summer time because there was always something going on then.

Erica picked up a piece of cheese and popped it in her mouth. For a long moment she sat there looking contemplative. He was silent, not wanting to push her. Whatever she needed to tell him, he'd let her do it in her own time.

As they sat there, he took her free hand and linked his fingers through hers. He needed to touch her, to have that extra connection. When she didn't say anything, that low grade panic increased. Apparently, he wasn't as patient as he thought. "Whatever's going on, whatever it is, you can tell me. Were you… seeing someone else?" he managed to choke out. "I mean, do I have competition?" Because if he did, he wasn't going to let her go without a fight.

She blinked, and he realized he'd definitely surprised her with the question. He wasn't sure if that was a good thing. Maybe she was surprised he'd guessed correctly?

Then she let out a giggle and shook her head. "I seriously can't believe you asked that. After what we shared together. I couldn't do that with you and be with someone else." Then her gaze went razor sharp with the intensity of only a she-wolf. "Why? Have you been seeing someone else in the last month?"

He snorted at the absurdity of her question. That was when he realized that his own fear had been stupid too. She wouldn't have been seeing someone else. "No." There was no one else for him. And he was pretty certain there never would be again. His wolf had decided and that was that.

She pushed out a shaky breath. "Okay then. Look," she said before suddenly turning away, bending over and getting sick.

Shit. He reached for her braid, pulling it out of the way as she emptied the contents of her stomach.

Panic punched through him as his mate got sick. It was pretty rare for their kind to get ill. So something must be seriously wrong. Oh God, was that why she'd come back?

As she sat back up, he handed her a napkin from the table.

With shaking hands, she wiped her mouth and gave him a watery smile.

Double shit. Now she was crying. "Let's go," he said, reaching for her hand as he stood.

Blinking at him in confusion, she frowned. "What?"

"We're going to see Abigail right now." Whatever was going on, their healer could take care of it.

She shook her head slightly. "Hudson, that's not necessary."

In response, he reached down and lifted her up into his arms. Oh, it was necessary. If she was sick, they were going to get her taken care of. He might be able to protect her from any outside threat, but he wasn't a damn doctor.

She started to protest, but paused when she saw some of his packmates staring at them.

"Don't worry about it, we'll take care of all this mess later," he said, worried that she was embarrassed that she'd thrown up. She had nothing to be embarrassed about. Getting sick wasn't her fault and he'd cleaned up enough messes from his packmates over the years that nothing fazed him anymore. He was just worried about her well-being.

"You're a lot more overbearing than I remember," she muttered.

"I told you I was a lot less civilized than you thought." There was no use fighting it anymore. "And you're mine. Which means I get to take care of you."

Now she watched him carefully as he strode around the crowd of packmates still carrying on with the party. He wasn't stopping for any of them. The last thing Erica needed right now was a bunch of nosy wolves. Even if they were concerned for her.

He knew for a fact that Abigail was up as she was taking care of a few of the wolves who'd gotten into a scuffle earlier. And even if she hadn't been, she would have wanted him to get her for anyone injured. Technically Erica wasn't injured but she'd just gotten sick and that couldn't be good.

His wolf was going into overprotective mode and he had to force himself to take a deep breath. Overreacting wouldn't do anyone any good. He always remained calm under pressure but apparently Erica brought out a new side to him.

He wasn't sure he liked it, but since he planned to mate with this woman, it was something he'd have to adjust to.

CHAPTER NINE

"Hudson, this is ridiculous. I'm fine." Erica gritted her teeth as they stopped in front of Abigail's cabin. The only reason she hadn't stopped him earlier was because she hadn't wanted to make a scene in front of his other packmates. But this had to end here and now. She wanted to tell Hudson she was pregnant alone.

"Then this shouldn't take long," he said, already opening the front door to Abigail's cabin as he set Erica on her feet.

"Shouldn't you knock—"

"Texted her on the way here. She said to come right on in."

She blinked. "How the hell did you do that?" While he was carrying her. He must have been stealth texting then because she hadn't noticed.

He just shrugged and as they stepped inside Abigail entered her living room from the kitchen.

"Hey guys. I hear you're not feeling well, Erica?" The petite Asian wolf's serene smile was in place as Hudson closed the door behind them.

"Ah... yeah. I wouldn't mind talking to you. In private." She didn't look at Hudson as she said it because she wasn't sure what his expression would be.

Abigail, an older wolf, didn't bat an eyelash as she nodded.

Hudson made a sort of strangled sound but didn't say anything else as Erica stepped closer to the healer.

"You want to talk in my office or the exam room?"

"Office is fine." She didn't need a checkup.

Once they were sitting inside, Abigail shut the sturdy door and said, "This room is soundproofed, so you've got true privacy. Hudson only texted that you'd gotten sick."

"Ah, yes."

"You're pregnant though. Not sick. And I take it he doesn't realize it yet?"

Erica blinked as she sat on the comfy loveseat. "Are you psychic too?"

Smiling in that serene way that made Erica want to tell Abigail all her secrets, the healer sat across from her in a high-backed chair. With no makeup on and her jet-black hair pulled back into two braids, she looked even younger than Erica. And Erica knew the healer was over a hundred.

"No, I can scent it." She touched one finger to her nose. "And before you ask, no, not all healers have that ability. But I do. It's deductive reasoning anyway. You came back here after a month, and Hudson said you threw up. I *might* have guessed anyway."

"Well then…" Erica wasn't sure what to say.

"Have you spoken to a healer back home?"

"I have."

"Are there any concerns?"

WOLF'S MATE | 63

"No."

"Okay then. If there's anything you need while you're here, just let me know."

"I will." It was Erica's instinct to ask her not to tell anyone but she knew Abigail wouldn't. She was a healer—and a doctor. Patient confidentiality and all that.

"I hope you stay," Abigail said as she stood. "He's missed you. A lot."

Erica joined her. "Really?" As soon as she asked the question she felt stupid.

But Abigail just laughed and shoved her hands in her jeans pockets. "Yeah. He's been pretty cranky without you. And I'm toning that down—he's kind of been an ass. And that's not like Hudson. He might be surly but he's not an ass."

"I'm… nervous about telling him."

Abigail's eyes widened slightly before she snorted. "I wouldn't worry about telling him."

Yeah, Erica wasn't so sure about that.

"If you want, tell him here before you head out. Just get it over with and you'll feel a lot better. I was planning to hit up the party for a bit anyway so go ahead and tell him. You'll have privacy."

"You're sure?"

"I promise."

"Okay, thank you." Even as tension built inside her, she was ready to just get it out.

After Abigail had left the house, Hudson shut the front door behind her and swiveled to face Erica, full-blown panic in his expression. "Is everything okay?"

Seeing him nervous put her even more off kilter. "Yes, but let's sit. And please lock the door." She didn't want any more damn interruptions.

He did as she asked then sat on the large leather couch in the living room, surprising her by pulling her into his lap. Somehow it made this harder, but she was getting it out no matter what. "I need to tell you something."

He stared at her expectantly, concern bright in his gaze.

She was so damn nervous. Better to just get it all out at once so she wasn't dropping two bombs. "I'm... pregnant. With twins."

Hudson sat there, staring at her for a long moment. So very long. She wasn't sure if time just seemed to stretch out because of her own nerves but holy crap, why wasn't he saying anything?

His grip tightened ever so slightly around her as he finally spoke. "Are you healthy? Are the babies?"

"Yes and yes."

"Good." He shoved out a harsh breath, all tension seeming to leave his shoulders. "You can move into my cabin as soon as possible. We'll add onto it if we need more space. Or just move into another, bigger one if that's easier." His words were coming out like machine gun fire, as if he was afraid to even breathe. "After we're officially mated, we'll—"

"Hudson! Breathe, please." She tried to wiggle out of his hold, but he just tightened his grip. "We're not getting mated." She paused as she realized he was actually growling and that his beautiful blue eyes were now pure wolf. "Are you seriously growling at me?"

"We are getting mated," he rasped out.

Annoyance flared inside her but she pushed it back down. She'd just dropped a huge, life-changing thing on him and he was trying to do the right thing. Or what he probably viewed as the right thing. "Look. We can have pups together and not be mated." It was pretty damn rare for that to happen but she wasn't going to get mated simply because she was pregnant.

"Our pups will have mated parents." He did that growling thing again.

It was weirdly adorable even if he was frustrating her with this nonsense. The idea of getting mated simply because she was pregnant was stupid, and insulting. If she ever did get mated, it would be for far different reasons. "Hudson—"

"Don't argue with me."

Taking a deep breath, she said, "Will you please let me stand? I need some space."

It very clearly took some willpower but he released his hold.

When she stood, she felt the loss of his touch, but was able to think clearer without his big, sexy hands on her. "Okay. Look. I came back here to tell in person that we're having twins. But I didn't expect you to start talking about mating."

He stood now, so many emotions on his handsome face she had no idea how to filter through any of them. "What's so wrong with being mated to me!"

"Nothing!" She found herself shouting right back. "But I'm not getting mated because you feel some sort of responsibility because I'm pregnant. And don't deny it, because if you'd wanted to get mated before, you'd have asked me!" Crap, now she couldn't stop shouting, all her emotions tumbling out like an avalanche.

"I asked you to stay here." Again with the growling.

Gah, this man was driving her crazy. "So what? You didn't ask me to mate you. You never said you had feelings for me. And you never offered to move to *my home* with me. You asked me to stay... for well, for what? More sex? And I'm not angry! I had a fun month with you. I'm just very clearly telling you that we're not getting mated. But that doesn't mean we can't be co-parents." Damn it, they had to get back on track. She didn't want to argue with him.

He clenched his jaw, watching her very carefully. "I did not ask you to stay. For. Just. Sex."

She didn't respond.

He pushed out a long breath, his expression annoyed. "You're from a different generation... I didn't want to scare you off."

A snort escaped before she could rein it in. "Did that sound better in your head?" Because it sounded pretty

WOLF'S MATE | 67

lame to her. And she'd expected more from him. Not this... garbage.

"It's the truth."

"So you're saying you wanted to mate me but... what, you didn't want to scare me off?" Now she laughed, but there was no humor in it. "That's the dumbest thing I've ever heard. When you decide to stop spouting off lies, come find me." She took a step toward the door and when he went to block her, she let out a growl. "Not tonight. We can talk tomorrow because I'm completely done with this stupid conversation. You're like a billion years old, if you'd wanted to mate you'd have done exactly what a wolf your age does! You'd have locked me down so fast. So do not come at me with more garbage like this. We can talk tomorrow." As more anger bubbled up inside her, her claws unleashed and she was pretty certain her wolf was in her eyes.

Not that she could ever actually scare him. But he stepped away from the door all the same.

Sure, he followed her all the way back to her cabin, but he kept his distance and didn't try to follow her inside. And he didn't break in, which he could have done. She felt a little bad ditching the party like that but really, the wolves probably wouldn't miss her much. A party was a party for a wolf.

Her heart was still racing as she stripped out of her clothes and got into the shower. "Didn't want to scare me off, what a bunch of bullshit," she muttered to herself as she angrily worked her hair into a lather.

Complete and utter garbage. And it was that particular lie that pissed her off more than anything. Why not just own the truth? Own that he was trying to get mated now because of the babies. Because he thought it was the right thing to do. Hurt lanced deep as she continued washing her hair. She'd hoped for... well, more than this tonight. Not lies.

She hadn't actually scented a lie coming off him, but she hadn't scented anything other than the turbulence of his emotions. Her own too. She'd been so worried about telling him the truth that her normal scent had been wild and tart.

What she needed now was some hot tea and sleep. Then she could talk to his dumb ass in the morning. If he spouted any more garbage off to her, she would not be liable for what she said or did.

Especially if she throat-punched him. She was hurting so badly right now, that it was a very real possibility.

As she let the hot water run down her body, some of her tension eased. Not much, but some. Because the disappointment that this was where she and Hudson now were... sucked. And as she stood there under the pulsing jets she couldn't help but think of the first time she'd known she'd fallen for Hudson. Truly and utterly.

Erica jumped up on the fence and sat next to Chelsea and a couple more of Hudson's packmates. "Is it always like this when the warriors spar?" For the most part she only had experience with her own pack and usually they sparred and practiced in their private gym. Mainly because they couldn't very well fight each other on the beach. Humans would definitely take exception to that.

"Sometimes we use the gym but with the weather being nice, everyone's outside today."

Erica found that she really liked being in Montana. Even if it was a whole lot colder than Alabama. She liked being outdoors and feeling as if she was a little more disconnected from humans. Not that she didn't like them, she did. A lot. One of her best friends was human but being surrounded solely by wolves, she could let her guard down more often.

"Is the whole pack here?" She glanced around to see wolves sitting on the surrounding fence like they were, while some were standing around and others looked as if they were... oh sweet flying puppies, were they placing bets?

"Nah, but Hudson told everyone that he could best anyone who challenged him today. He pretty much threw down the gauntlet."

As second-in-command he was strong, but that was a pretty bold statement to make. Not that she doubted he could take on anyone he so chose to fight. The man was built like a linebacker and the power that rolled off of him was palpable. Not to mention he had experience—he'd been in some of the former vampire-werewolf wars over a century ago. "Is that normal?"

Chelsea snorted as she shook her head. Then she tilted her chin to the left of them. Erica followed the direction and saw Hudson striding into the makeshift ring—aka, the horse training area—with another shifter not far behind. Hudson looked at her and winked, and she felt it all the way to her toes.

"I swear to God I have never seen him like this. If he was a freaking peacock, his feathers would be on display for you right now. Seriously, he normally fights and spars with a lot more clothing—and he doesn't wink at people like a freaking pup," the female said to her.

"I'm not complaining," Erica murmured as her gaze tracked over all of his exposed skin, enjoying the way his arm muscles and chest flexed as he strode forward. Yeah, her friend was right. Hudson was most definitely showing off for her.

And that was incredibly hot. Sure, she'd dated a few wolves in college and it wasn't as if she was a virgin, but Hudson made her feel special. He made her feel as if she was the only she-wolf that existed. And she loved that the big bad two-hundred-year-old second-in-command was putting on a show for her. "I feel like I should have gotten popcorn to watch this," she murmured.

Chelsea giggled. "I'm going to place a bet on Hudson. You want in on this action?"

Laughing, Erica shook her head. She wasn't going to bet on him. It felt wrong somehow even if she had no doubt that he was going to win.

"That's all right, I'll grab you a beer."

Erica nodded as her new friend headed off to take care of business.

Immediately her gaze was drawn back to Hudson and his powerful body. All she could think about was how he'd pinned her up against the wall of his bedroom not two hours ago, how he'd made her come twice, made her moan out his name each time. The man had wicked, long fingers. Not to mention his mouth. That very wicked mouth.

She was vaguely aware that Chelsea returned and placed a beer in her hand, but all her focus was on Hudson now that the first sparring session had started. He got the guy pinned and tapping out in less than sixty seconds. Then the next wolf jumped in. Then the next. Soon he was facing off with four of his packmates and for a brief moment she felt worried for him even though she knew this was a sparring session. No one would die, but he could still get hurt.

A moment later she realized that she had nothing to be worried about because the man was magic. He was all lethal efficiency, his moves perfectly executed as he knocked back wolf after wolf with incredible force. And she was under the impression that he was actually holding back a little.

She couldn't believe she was getting turned on as she watched him fight. She wasn't a warrior and though she wasn't squeamish about fighting and bloodshed, not like humans were, sometimes the brutality of her kind could get to her. Not so now. Watching him had her heart rate skyrocketing and other parts getting... warmer.

"Oh my gosh, I can smell your pheromones from here," Chelsea whispered. "You better give that man the prize he deserves after this session." Chelsea's voice was light and teasing as she laughed into her beer.

Erica might have responded, she wasn't sure. It was hard to be sure of anything when she couldn't tear her gaze away from Hudson.

In that moment, she realized that she'd completely fallen for him. Head over heels. And she wasn't sure what the hell to do about it. She'd be going home soon. They agreed that this was fun and casual.

Now... She wanted more than casual. So much more.

Erica shook herself out of the memory, forcing herself to remain in the present. She'd come here with no expectations. Or at least that was what she'd told herself. But maybe she'd been lying to herself? Maybe she wanted everything, including his heart.

CHAPTER TEN

Hudson knocked on the door to the guest cabin, his heart rate jacked up at the thought of seeing Erica. He had to keep it together this morning—even if he wanted to insist that they get mated right the hell now. But that would be the wrong move.

Clearly.

Especially after the argument last night. Damn it, he should have just been honest with her last month and made it clear that he wanted her forever.

A moment later, Erica opened the door wearing pajamas but she was wide awake. She eyed him warily.

He held up a bag of treats he'd snagged from Leah. "I've got muffins, pastries and cookies."

She sniffed the air slightly, took the bag and stepped back to let him in.

"How are you feeling this morning? Any sickness?" He wished he'd been able to talk to her more last night, to tell her how damn happy he was that they were having children. As in plural. Instead he'd lost his mind because he'd been consumed with the need to make things official, to mate with her.

"I'm okay. No nausea—it seems to come whenever it pleases and with no warning. But I've had some crackers this morning and they've stayed down."

"There are some plain muffins in the bag—I didn't tell Leah you're pregnant. But I asked for something simple. She said she'd give you anything you wanted after the manicure you gave her." He was absolutely certain she'd charmed his entire pack. Just as she'd charmed him.

"Thank you. So, you want some coffee? I'm not drinking any but I can make you a pot."

"I'm good." He shoved his hands in his pockets, feeling awkward. "Can we sit down and talk?"

"Oh, yeah, of course. Ah, kitchen okay? I was just about to make some raspberry tea."

He nodded and followed her into the kitchen. He was silent as she moved around the kitchen, her hands shaking slightly. Part of him wanted to offer to help but he could tell she wanted to keep her hands busy. He was desperate to put her at ease, to tell her exactly how he felt and that he wanted to start their life together.

"So… twins? How do you know that so soon?" God, the thought of her growing bigger with his kids had him all twisted up inside. In the best way possible.

"The healer I saw back home was certain. She could tell. Said it was one of her gifts. Abigail guessed I was pregnant before I told her." She snorted softly as she set the kettle on the stove. "She was so certain I thought she might be psychic."

Even though his instinct was to pace right now, he forced himself to sit at the rectangular table by the window. "Is there anything we need to be worried about? Like… I don't know. I know nothing about pregnancies."

Sure, his packmates had pups but he'd never been involved in any of their pregnancies.

"No. Or my healer didn't think so. And I'm about two
months along. Which means…"

"Wow." That meant they had five months to prepare
because shifter pregnancies were shorter than human
ones. It didn't seem like a long time either. Soon she'd be
showing, probably in another month or so. When shifters 'popped', it was sudden, almost overnight. At least
they had another month before announcing anything if
she wanted to wait. He kind of wanted to beat his chest
and tell the whole fucking pack that his woman was
pregnant. With twins. Which, yeah, made him feel even
more uncivilized. But he didn't much care.

"Yeah, right? I'm feeling a little overwhelmed."

Screw it. He wasn't just going to sit here. Moving
across the kitchen, he leaned against the counter next to
her, taking one of her hands in his. "I'm going to be there
for you for everything."

She sighed slightly. "I know. Last night I feel like
things got a little out of hand."

"I shouldn't have started talking about mating right
away. For the record, I want to get mated. Not because
you're pregnant but because I love you. I want a family
with you."

She blinked.

But he kept going. "I won't pressure you. Not now
anyway. But I'm putting it out there so you know how I
feel. No lies. Just the truth. I also know we have a lot of

stuff to worry about, like where we're going to raise our kids. And a bunch of other kid and pregnancy stuff I've never thought of."

A minute dragged out as she stared at him, the scents rolling off her wild and untamed. Fuck. Just like that he was hard. No, scratch that. He was generally turned on around Erica. Of course, it was completely inappropriate timing right now.

"You just dropped a lot on me. Can we…" She turned back to the stove as the kettle whistled.

Moving quickly, he took it off the burner even as he switched off the stovetop. "Can we what?"

"Maybe not talk about anything us-related today? Just… I don't know how to respond to what you just said."

He gritted his teeth while his back was to her, trying not to be so damn hurt that she hadn't responded to the fact that he loved her. He wasn't lying. She had to scent it. And she hadn't reciprocated.

"Okay, I lied. I guess I do still want to talk about us. Can I ask you something else?" Erica sat at the kitchen table as he poured her drink. Though only a few feet separated them, he felt as if the Grand Canyon did.

The way they were acting around each other wasn't exactly like strangers, but there was a wall between them. And he wanted to tear it down. "Of course."

"So… you say you love me—"

"I do," he growled. "I should have told you sooner. Should have done a lot of things sooner."

She nodded slowly as she continued. "Once, after you'd been dealing with the teenagers over something, you made a comment about not wanting to bring pups into this world. And you sounded really serious. I... assumed you were serious."

As he set the steaming mug in front of her, he tried to remember that conversation. "I... might have been serious at the time. But I want kids with you. I want everything with you."

"Really?" She sounded far too shocked by this.

"Yes, really. Erica... this is happening way faster than I ever thought. And having kids... does kind of terrify me. But the thought of being mated to you, of having kids with you, *that* doesn't scare me."

She was silent again, looking down into her mug and he wished he knew what she was thinking. When she said, "okay," he wasn't sure what it was in reference to and he wasn't going to ask. He wanted to push so damn hard, but she was freaking pregnant and... he was in completely new territory.

When his phone buzzed in his pocket, he contemplated crushing it under his boot. Damn it, damn it, damn it. Nope. He was not dealing with any shit today.

"Before you murder your phone, at least check the message," she murmured, a hint of the Erica he knew well trickling through as she smiled.

When he checked the message, he wished he'd just smashed the damn thing. "My brother is meeting with our neighboring alpha. Wants me at one of the border lines just in case anything stupid happens."

"Is this about all that petty vandalism?"

He nodded. "Maybe. Honestly, we're not sure what's going on. Our neighbor, Alex, has always been a good alpha. Has a strong pack. The last couple months, however, things have been strained."

"Go take care of it. I'm not going anywhere. Promise."

He wanted to stay. He really did. But... he couldn't let his brother or his pack down for this. If his brother was meeting with another alpha, he had to be out on the ground ready to move into action if necessary. "I'll have my phone on me if you need me. And you know where Abigail is so if you need—"

"I'll be fine," she said, standing with him. "I'll probably just take a hot bath and—"

He groaned at the thought of her naked in a tub and realized that sound had been far too loud and sexual.

Her eyes widened. "That thought turns you on?"

"Anything you do turns me on," he murmured, stepping closer. Fuck. His wolf was going crazy, torn with the need to take care of pack business and with the need to take care of his mate. When he scented just a hint of her lust through the fog of his mind, he took a deep breath. "If you touch yourself in the bath, think of me."

"I will," she whispered.

"When I get back, let me get you off." It had been too long since he'd tasted her.

"Only if I get you off first."

Oh hell. He was definitely a goner for her. Unable to find his voice, he simply nodded and brushed his lips over hers, the action more tender than he'd ever been. Though he wanted to deepen the kiss, to plunder her mouth, he held back.

For now. And as he strode out of the cabin, he knew there were things he needed to think about. Things he'd been ignoring since last night. Like the fact that he hadn't offered to go live with her.

He'd simply never thought of it and he wasn't sure what that said about him. His pack was here. His life was here. But hers was in Alabama. When he'd asked her to stay with him, he'd meant it with the intention of getting her to move here eventually. To become his. But he'd never considered moving across the country.

And he should have. Hell, he definitely should have. Things weren't just about him anymore. Not only about his wants or needs. If Erica wanted him to move, he would. He knew it would be difficult. But he'd sacrifice anything for her.

Now he just needed to convince her of that truth.

CHAPTER ELEVEN

Erica shut the cabin door behind her, immediately feeling better as she drank in the fresh fall air. Though it was more like winter to her southern sensibilities even if there was no snow on the ground yet. She really loved it here, the weather was great, there was room to roam whenever her wolf wanted and... Hudson was here.

Hudson.

The wolf who'd told her he loved. If he'd tried to say it last night she might have thought he was full of it, but she was starting to believe him. She loved him too. But she'd been too afraid to say the words out loud.

The conversation they'd had before he got called away a couple hours ago replayed in her mind, over and over. He'd been serious about everything.

Which meant she'd had some pre-conceived ideas— based on things as she knew them—that had turned out to be wrong. Apparently, he really had been trying to go slow. She wasn't sure why because she kinda liked the caveman, uncivilized version of Hudson. And she wanted a wolf who chased after her, who made it clear that he wanted to mate her. Not someone who dragged their feet.

Now she had that.

And she was freaking terrified. Yes, she believed him, but things were happening at warp speed. And okay, she was pregnant. With twins. And she was scared. Her parents had died when she'd been young and she'd more or less been raised by the pack. Erica had no complaints either. Her pack was amazing.

Except now... she wanted to leave them. Sure, she'd been traveling the last year but it had been with the knowledge that she'd be going home eventually. Now she wanted to move *here*, to be with Hudson. Because she loved him and wanted to raise kids with him. No one would view it as a betrayal, she knew that. It just felt... She sighed. It was simply a whole lot of change on top of the huge change she was facing that made her feel completely off kilter.

And way too deep in her own thoughts, she realized, as she glanced around the mostly quiet forest. She'd just started walking, not taking a particular path when she'd left the cabin. Now... she wasn't quite sure where she was, but that was only because she didn't know the layout of the property. She'd be able to find her way back once she was ready. Her wolf was a great tracker.

Now, however, she decided to keep walking and enjoy being outdoors. The sun was high in the sky, warming her face even as a sharp breeze wrapped around her.

She paused as she heard the sound of male and female voices nearby. She liked all of Hudson's packmates, or the ones she'd met so far at least. Picking up her pace, she followed the voices and smiled when she saw what were definitely teenagers fixing a fence.

"Hey, guys," she called out.

The three pups, two males and one female, turned to look at her. When they saw her, one of the guys held up a hand to wave. Then she heard… a growling sound.

Turning, she saw a huge, gray and brown wolf racing through the forest toward her. It was impossible to truly know a wolf's mood while in shifter form but Hudson looked pretty angry.

"Shit," one of the pups muttered, and by the time she'd turned around, they'd all shifted, shredding their clothes and were sprinting away.

"Hudson!" she called out as he raced past her.

He paused, looked at her, then in the direction the pups had gone, before turning back to her. Then he let out another growl. Whatever the pups had done couldn't have been that bad.

Finally, he shifted to his human form, all his brown and gray fur receding to be replaced by a pissed off, naked man. "Did they hurt you?" He was in front of her before she'd blinked, cupping her cheek with one hand and placing the other protectively on her stomach.

In that moment, she melted way too much for him. "Ah, the kids fixing the fence? No."

"They're not from our pack and they're not fixing the damn fence. They were tearing it down."

"Oh. They're still kids." Stupid ones, apparently, if they'd decided to mess with the Kendrick pack. But that was kind of the definition of being a kid. You sometimes did dumb stuff. Though screwing with another wolf's property was really, really stupid. "Look, what's going on?" She placed a hand on his bare chest to find his heart racing out of control. Something more had to have happened.

A few other wolves ran up to them, coming from the direction Hudson had just come. He simply pointed in the direction the kids had run and the little pack took off.

"Caught some movement on the sensors we set up and when we headed this way I caught your scent." His breathing was harsh as he continued talking, his eyes still wolf. "I could scent the intruders mixed with yours and my wolf went crazy. I sprinted ahead of my packmates to get to you. I thought you were in danger."

On instinct she pulled him into a hug. "I was never in any danger," she murmured against his chest, knowing that wouldn't matter to him, but still trying to soothe him all the same. She'd be a wreck if she thought he was in danger too.

His grip tightened but he didn't respond, just held her.

"Are you going to tell me what's really going on?" He'd talked about border security issues in vague terms. "I know I'm not part of your pack—"

He instantly pulled back to look down at her—and she had to force herself not to turn into a perv and eye the rest of his very naked self. "I'm not holding anything back from you. Like I said before, my brother is meeting with the neighboring alpha." He glanced over at the planks from the fence lying haphazardly on the hard ground. "This is probably nothing more than petty vandalism, but it's stopping today." There was a menacing note in his voice that sent a shiver down her spine.

Not because she was worried about herself at all—but that other pack was in serious trouble. "Should I head back to my cabin?"

He started to nod, then shook his head. "No. The rest of my packmates are headed back. I can scent them," he added when she gave him a curious look. "Once they get here we'll all head back. Then we're going to meet with my brother and Alex, the other alpha. Did you see the faces of who did this?" he asked.

She nodded. "I can identify them if that's what you're asking."

He nodded before brushing his lips over hers. Then he shifted back to wolf form as his packmates returned. He barked out something that they understood before they raced off into the woods.

Hudson simply nudged her instead of running off with his packmates, so she fell in step with him. The way he'd reacted when he'd thought she was in danger pretty much erased all the worry she had. She was going to tell him exactly how she felt.

* * *

Hudson tamped down his aggression as he watched his brother and Alex talk. Both had their arms crossed over their chests as they faced off with each other, standing on opposite sides of the invisible line that ran down

86 | KATIE REUS

the middle of their property line. They were speaking too low for either of the packs to hear what was being said.

As a cool breeze kicked up, Hudson wrapped his arm around Erica's shoulders even tighter. He'd read that pregnant shifters felt the elements more since their bodies were slightly more vulnerable. He didn't look down at her, however. Didn't take his gaze off the cluster of Alex's pack standing behind the alpha.

Nothing separated them. Not really. And a property line meant nothing. Clearly it didn't, not to some of Alex's packmates.

When Malcolm looked over and nodded once at Hudson, he squeezed Erica. She fell in step with him to meet the two alphas. As they walked, Hudson noticed that Alex's second-in-command not so subtly stepped forward as well, her eyes pure wolf as she watched Hudson for any wrong moves.

"This is Erica, she's visiting our pack," Malcolm said, his voice polite and civil as he motioned to her. "Erica, this is Alex Lincoln, my neighbor and alpha of the Lincoln pack."

Alex nodded once at her, his smile polite. "It's a pleasure to meet you. I'm acquainted with your alpha, Grant."

Erica smiled and nodded but didn't say anything else.

"Malcolm tells me you saw some of my wolves tearing down one of his fences."

"I saw three wolves. I don't know if they're yours or not. But I can describe them or just pick them out if your entire pack is here."

His jaw tightened but he nodded once. "What do they look like?"

Erica gave a basic description and before she'd even finished Alex's second was growling. She turned and snapped out three names. A moment later, three wolves shuffled forward, looking at the ground as they walked. They were staring so hard at the earth it was clear they wanted it to open up and swallow them.

"That's them," Erica said quietly.

"They're not working alone," Malcolm snapped out. "Because more than simply three wolves have been destroying my pack's property the last two months. This ends now or we're no longer allies."

Alex nodded once, his gray eyes filled with a stone-cold anger. "It will end tonight." He took a deep breath, paused as if considering his words before he looked at Malcolm. "There's a very small group of wolves in my pack who think they have what it takes to run the pack—to challenge me." He snorted. "I've been patient with them, trying to allow them to exert their dominance without crushing their spirit. One of them is related to me. I'm done." His wolf peered out at them as he continued, raising his voice. "And if anyone does anything else to your land or your packmates after tonight, they're yours to deal with. They will not have my protection." Much quieter he added, "I'll contact you once I'm done dealing with them. I'm… sorry. I should have cut this off sooner. The kid who thinks he can take over is a cousin. Not an excuse though, and I own my responsibility in this."

Spoken like a true alpha.

Malcolm nodded and held out a hand. "No worries. Handle your pack. We're good as far as I'm concerned—as long as you take care of things now."

That was that. Malcolm turned and motioned toward the rest of the pack, who quickly dispersed, heading deeper into the woods and back toward their cabins.

"That was… interesting," Erica murmured, looking up at Hudson.

He lifted a shoulder. "Alex will be cleaning house tonight. I don't foresee a problem after this. Listen, I need to talk to my brother about some pack stuff," he said as they headed back toward the line of trees. "I won't be long. Do you mind waiting for me at the cabin?"

"I'll be there." The smile she gave him was soft and sweet. He didn't want to read too much into it, but things seemed different between them now.

Better. Like they'd been before. Now he needed to talk to his brother about a big change. And he knew exactly how it was going to go over.

CHAPTER TWELVE

"What's up?" Malcolm asked as he shut his office door behind him and faced Hudson.

"I might be transferring to the Kincaid pack. I need to talk to Erica, see what she really wants. If she wants to move, I'm going with her." It tore Hudson open to say the words aloud. Words he'd never thought to utter— that he'd be leaving his pack. His brother's pack. *His* pack. One he'd been part of for over a hundred years after Malcolm decided to break out on his own. Not all family members worked and lived together like he and his brother did.

"I... did not expect that." Malcolm's jaw tightened as he strode over to one of his cabinets. He pulled out an aged bottle of whisky and poured the amber liquid into two tumblers.

They might not feel the effects of alcohol like humans did, but they certainly enjoyed a single malt Scottish whisky.

His brother handed him a glass and clinked it once. "Whatever you decide, I'll support you."

He nodded once, his throat tight. He hadn't expected any less, but it was still difficult to think about actually leaving. Though that was all lessened by the fact that he'd be doing it with Erica. And when he thought of her, most of the tension left his chest.

"I haven't told anyone yet. We haven't…" He cleared his throat. "Erica's pregnant with twins."

Malcolm blinked, then grinned, his reaction immediate and genuine as he pulled Hudson into a tight hug. "Congratulations, brother!"

Hudson squeezed Malcolm once before stepping back, his own elation pouring through him. He was going to be a father. Something that was a privilege for any wolf. Having pups was harder for them than humans and the fact that he was having two, and with the woman he loved? Yeah, he couldn't be happier. "Thank you. Until she says it's okay, we're going to hold off on telling anyone else."

His brother nodded once, then plucked the glass from Hudson's hand. "Go be with your she-wolf."

He didn't have to tell Hudson twice. He barely remembered the walk back to Erica's cabin. When he got there, he knew she wasn't inside even before he knocked. Her scent wasn't fresh enough and he couldn't hear any movement inside regardless.

Frowning, he pulled out his cell phone as he stalked back to his cabin. But she didn't pick up. She wouldn't have left though, would she? No. He refused to believe that. She'd probably just got caught up with one of his packmates doing something else. They all adored her, not that he could blame them.

Still, he couldn't fight that low-grade panic humming through him. Last time when he'd returned to his cabin and found her gone he might have broken some things. And hurt his fists. Fuck. If she had left, she wouldn't have been able to go far. As he raced up the steps to his cabin, he pulled out his phone again and called the pack's pilot.

No way in hell was he letting his female go again.

* * *

Erica was nervous as she set everything up in Hudson's cabin. He'd asked her to go back to 'the cabin' and wait for him and she was pretty sure he'd meant the guest one. Well, she'd decided to head to his instead. To make things crystal clear. She knew where she belonged.

He'd asked her to move here, been frank that he loved her and wanted to mate with her. It was time to step up her game, to show him exactly how much he meant to her. She'd been trying to protect her heart before she'd left.

Now that he'd laid himself bare, there was no more need. And if she kept pulling back she might lose the best thing that had ever happened to her. The man she loved.

Okay she didn't actually think she would lose him. Now that he'd told her how he felt, how he truly felt, it was as if he'd let free some primal side of himself and she had a feeling that if she tried to run from him, he'd follow. Not that she would run.

Not again.

Maybe she should have stayed rather than run before. At this point she'd never know exactly what the right choice was. All she knew was that she loved Hudson. And she wanted to be with him all the time.

What she was doing right now might be completely cheeseball, but she didn't care as she tossed the last handful of rose petals on his giant bed. She'd never done anything remotely romantic for a guy but with Hudson, she wanted to get this right.

Though she was pretty certain that if she just waited in his bed naked for him, that was all it would take. Still, she wanted tonight to be special.

When the front door slammed open she nearly jumped a foot. She hurried down the hallway to the front of the cabin. Chelsea had helped her earlier with getting tealight candles—Hudson had none—flowers and some other stuff. Maybe she'd come back. Her eyes widened when she saw Hudson standing in the doorway, his eyes pure wolf.

He blinked once when he saw her, and then she was looking at the man again. Not the animal. "You're here."

She nodded, smiling. "I am."

He kicked the door shut behind him, making her jump again, and then he was standing in front of her, having moved faster than she could blink. "You weren't at your cabin. Thought you'd left."

"I'm not going anywhere," she whispered, hating that he thought that for even a moment.

He glanced around briefly, taking in all the surfaces covered in candles and rose petals before zeroing in on her again. His big hands settled on her hips as he pulled her so that she was flush against his body.

It was impossible to miss his hard erection. She rubbed against him as she linked her fingers together behind his neck. Nope, not going anywhere at all.

"Good. If you run, I'll chase you down," he murmured, his voice dropping an octave. "Which is what I should have done a month ago."

"I would have liked that." She-wolves could be a picky bunch. They liked their mates to chase them down, to make a public claim. Maybe it was in their DNA.

"I'm not letting you go again… and I'm moving with you. To live with you and your pack."

She blinked, some of the haze of lust fading. "What?"

"I just talked with my brother and—"

She was shaking her head before he'd finished. "No. I don't want that and I don't think you do either. I'll move here—I *want* to."

His jaw tightened even as his grip on her hips did. "You made a really good point before, about how I didn't even offer to move. And you're right. This isn't a hollow offer. I'm moving—"

"Nope." She smiled when he simply scowled at her. "I do appreciate the offer and I think I needed to hear it, but no. I love my pack. Well, my soon-to-be former pack. But I love you more. And you're already established here and—"

"What?"

"Yes, it makes more sense. And I love it here, love being able to run free all the time. Plus, there's an opportunity for me to start my own business here and—"

"No, I meant… you love me?"

She blinked. "*Yes.* So much. I realized I'd fallen for you that day you showed off for me, fighting all your packmates in the ring." He'd been such a beast that day and it had been insanely sexy. She loved him more than she could probably put into words. Which was why she'd set up all this stuff at his place. To show him what he meant to her.

His mouth came down on hers, hungry and dominating. And everything else ceased to exist as he hoisted her up. She wrapped her legs around his waist as he carried her somewhere.

Flowers, candles and the bottle of champagne she'd managed to snag were forgotten as her back bumped into something hard.

The wall.

His hands slid up under her sweater, his big, callused fingers teasing over her skin as he moved higher, higher. He shoved her bra up until one of his hands cupped her breast, teasing her nipple in a rhythmic, maddening pattern. And he was just teasing one nipple, leaving the other one all needy.

God, she wished he had more than two hands. The ache between her legs grew as he slowly lifted her sweater over her head. Then her bra was discarded just as quickly.

When he stared down at her bare breasts, she felt that look all the way to her core. He was all heat and hunger and it was a wonder she didn't combust on the spot. She knew what it felt like to have him thrusting inside her and she was desperate for it. For him. And he was just pausing, taking his sweet time while she was ready to climb the damn walls.

She dug her fingers into his shoulders, a silent plea. Finally, mercifully, he dipped a head to one breast even as he cupped the other, teasing them both with his tongue and fingers.

And there it was. A tiny modicum of relief. Not much, however. Because the ache between her legs was growing as his teasing increased.

She rolled her hips against him, hating the clothing remaining between them. Why was he even dressed at all? The man should be naked all the time.

As he sucked one nipple between his teeth, she yanked at his sweater, forcing him to lift his head. She missed his mouth on her, but she took the opportunity to tug his sweater up and off. She tossed it away—careful not to throw it on a candle. Though even fire wouldn't stop her now.

Nothing would.

The rest of their clothes came off in a rush as they stumbled toward the bedroom. She didn't care where they finally ended up, but let out a laugh as her back once again hit something.

Soft this time. The bed.

He shoved a handful of flower petals out of the way as he caged her in with his big body. All his muscles were pulled taut as he looked down at her, breathing hard.

She could easily get lost in his blue eyes.

"If I get too rough, just tell me," he rasped out.

She cupped his face in her hands and pulled his mouth to hers. The second their mouths fused, another rush of heat let loose inside her.

Grinding her body against his, she moaned at the feel of his cock rubbing against her slick folds. She was pretty certain he was going to tease her and was more than okay with that.

When he cupped her mound, he let out a moan of his own as he slid two fingers inside her. She was soaking wet and it was all because of him.

Slowly, he began stroking inside her, in and out, before adding a third finger, stretching her, readying her.

The last month without him had been pure torture. Knowing what she was missing—craving it—had made it even harder to be separated from him. He'd gotten under her skin and wasn't going anywhere.

He was hers. Forever.

Sliding her hands down his back and only stopping when she reached his perfectly sculpted ass, she squeezed hard.

He groaned again, rolling his hips against her even as he continued stroking.

She wanted more than his fingers though. "More," she growled against his mouth. So much more. They'd waited long enough.

He pulled back only slightly to look down at her, his eyes darker than usual, the heat there unmistakable. Then he nipped once at her bottom lip before turning her onto her knees.

They were doing this, officially mating. Every part of her cried out for it, needed it. No matter what she'd tried to tell herself before, that she could have co-parented without this intimate bond between them, she didn't want to. Could she have? Yeah. But she wanted everything from Hudson.

To be mates and teammates as well. Because that was what they were becoming. A team.

"I love you so much," he growled as he grasped her hips, pulling her ass flush against him.

Her inner walls clenched as she waited for him to fill her. Wanting to tease him right back, she wiggled against his hard length, laughing lightly as he growled again. "Hurry up then."

He wouldn't be rushed, though. Taking his sweet time, he leaned over her, kissed down her spine, leaving a trail of heat with each touch, as if he was branding her. At least that was what it felt like.

When he nipped at her butt, she groaned, clutching the sheets beneath them, wanting to tear right through them. No more teasing.

Maybe he read her mind, or more likely, he was just as ready as she was, because when he grabbed her hips again, she knew what was coming.

He slid a hand between her legs from behind, rubbing his finger along her folds again, testing how wet she was. Then he was inside her, stretching and filling her and already pushing her to the edge with each hard stroke.

Thick and long, his cock was perfect. As if he'd been made for her. She pushed back into him each time he thrust, getting lost in the sensation of her mate filling her.

Her inner walls tightened faster and faster around him the closer she pushed to the edge of orgasm. And close she was, teetering on the brink of it. All her muscles pulled tight as she waited for that inevitable release he always brought out of her.

When he slid his hand from her hip, moving at molasses speed until he reached her mound, she was practically shaking. Then he teased her clit and it was all over. Her climax started building, faster and faster. His little strokes were teases at first, the rhythm driving her crazy. As he increased the pressure, her orgasm hit full force, the pleasure punching out to all her nerve endings.

He scored the spot where her shoulder and neck met with his canines, making his claim complete even as he growled against her skin. "Mine."

The possessive word was unmistakable, sending another rush of heat through her, making her nipples bead even tighter. The bite of pain on her skin was mixed with the pleasure of knowing they were bonded for life. They were officially mates.

"Yours," she rasped out, knowing he needed the confirmation. She was his. And he was hers. No doubt about it now.

When he started coming inside her, she couldn't help it. Her claws unleashed and she shredded his sheets as she lost control. Knowing that they'd cemented their bond set something free inside her.

"Hudson." She groaned out his name as he grasped her hips hard now, emptying himself inside her.

Finally, they collapsed against the tattered sheets, but she wasn't remotely tired. Turning so that she could face him, she wrapped her arms and legs around him, burying her face against his neck.

He held her close, inhaling deeply and she knew he was scenting their mating. Because she was as well. It was overwhelming, making her lightheaded.

"I'm ready for round two," she whispered. This had only taken the edge off and now she was keyed up for more. She'd heard about this happening after mating. It was as if someone had shot her up with adrenaline.

To her surprise, his body shook as he laughed. Pulling back to look at her, he said, "I think we can manage that."

"I've got champagne chilling—non-alcoholic." She could go for some bubbly now too.

"How about I drink it off your body?"

Her inner walls tightened at his softly growled words. Oh yeah, she liked that idea a whole lot.

EPILOGUE

One year later

Erica strode into the gym, wondering what on earth Hudson could have brought their babies here for. But she'd gotten home after a half-day at the salon to find a note on the kitchen table. Which she found suspicious since her mate could have simply texted her—until she saw him going toe-to-toe with his brother.

Watching the two males from the sidelines were another two warriors holding Hunter and Evan.

"What are you doing?" she asked, coming to stand in between the two of them.

Both shifters startled a little, clearly not having scented or seen her. "Ah…"

"Hudson wanted his boys to see him fight. Said they needed to start early."

Oh, sweet flying puppies. Rolling her eyes, she took Evan in her arms since he was wide awake and making grabby hands for her. Hunter, thankfully was asleep. Usually her two boys were awake at the same time and clamoring for her attention.

Erica rubbed her nose over Evan's cheek, inhaling his sweet, perfect baby scent. She still couldn't believe she was a mother. To twins. Some days it felt surreal, but she wouldn't give up her family, this life, for anything.

"When's the last time you changed them?" she asked.

"An hour ago," the two males said, practically in unison.

"Is that how long these two pups have been sparring?" she asked, motioning to her mate and their alpha—who were definitely not pups even if they acted like it on occasion.

"Just about. I swear Hudson timed it perfectly so he wouldn't have to change their diapers. As soon as Malcolm and he started going at it, this one just let loose. Then Evan followed." The younger wolf shuddered.

Yep, she believed it. Babies were pooping machines. It was insane how much came out of them. When Hunter started to stir, she called out. "Hudson! Time to wrap this up."

He turned to look at her and Malcolm took the opportunity to tackle him—and then do the worst victory dance she'd ever seen.

Hudson swiped Malcolm's ankles out from under him before rolling over and jumping up. Then he was in front of her and the babies in a second, kissing her soundly as Evan made gurgling sounds. "Missed you today," he murmured.

"I can see that," she said dryly.

"I've gotta keep in shape—the kids were impressed."

Evan let out another gurgling sound, as if in agreement.

"See?"

She snickered and kissed Evan on the nose. "Uh huh. If you want to hit the showers, I can take the boys back."

"I'll shower at home," he said, scooping Hunter up from their packmate. "And I invited Malcolm and some of the guys over for dinner tonight. Figured I'd fire up the grill."

"Sounds good. I asked some of the girls over too." Mostly packmates from the salon so they were sure to have a full house. Which meant a lot of packmates holding and cuddling their babies.

His eyes held a glint of hunger. "Maybe we can sneak away for some alone time while everyone's fawning all over the boys."

"You're terrible," she murmured. "We can't ditch our own dinner."

"Wanna bet?" Hudson cuddled Hunter close as they headed across the huge stretch of property toward their new cabin.

They'd ended up moving to a slightly bigger cabin so the boys could have their own rooms if they ever decided they wanted them. For now, however, they shared a room. Even if they ended up sleeping with Hudson and Erica every night anyway in matching bassinets. Soon they'd be too big and would have to move to their cribs. Something she was dreading a little.

She'd gotten so used to having them right next to her, it was going to be weird to have their room back to themselves.

Well, weird and probably good even if having babies sure hadn't slowed her and Hudson down any. Once the healer had given her the go-ahead to have sex again, they'd gotten very creative about when and where they got intimate. Luckily, they lived near a bunch of packmates who loved babysitting.

"Oh, I got a call from one of my old packmates," she said as they stepped into their cabin. Warmth immediately surrounded them. "She said she wants to come out and visit for a couple weeks."

"Malcolm won't care."

"I didn't think so, but will you ask him for me?"

"No problem," he murmured before dropping a light kiss on her lips. "Gonna change this one, then get in the shower."

Smiling, she watched his sexy backside as he strode away, Hunter held carefully in his arms. She hadn't realized it was possible, but she'd fallen even harder for Hudson after they'd become parents.

Seeing him in protective dad mode was pretty much the sexiest thing ever. Sometimes he could go overboard, but she was more than okay with it. The life they'd created together was something she'd always wanted and never actually allowed herself to imagine. He could go overboard on the protectiveness and love all he wanted. She loved every second of it.

Thank you for reading Wolf's Mate I really hope you enjoyed it. If you don't want to miss any future releases, please feel free to join my newsletter. Find the signup link on my website: https://www.katiereus.com

Red Stone Security Series
No One to Trust
Danger Next Door
Fatal Deception
Miami, Mistletoe & Murder
His to Protect
Breaking Her Rules
Protecting His Witness
Sinful Seduction
Under His Protection
Deadly Fallout
Sworn to Protect
Secret Obsession
Love Thy Enemy
Dangerous Protector
Lethal Game

Redemption Harbor Series
Resurrection
Savage Rising
Dangerous Witness
Innocent Target
Hunting Danger

The Serafina: Sin City Series
First Surrender
Sensual Surrender
Sweetest Surrender
Dangerous Surrender

Deadly Ops Series
Targeted
Bound to Danger
Chasing Danger (novella)
Shattered Duty
Edge of Danger
A Covert Affair

O'Connor Family Series
Merry Christmas, Baby
Tease Me, Baby
It's Me Again, Baby
Mistletoe Me, Baby

Non-series Romantic Suspense
Running From the Past
Dangerous Secrets
Killer Secrets
Deadly Obsession
Danger in Paradise
His Secret Past

Linked books
Retribution
Tempting Danger

Paranormal Romance
Destined Mate
Protector's Mate
A Jaguar's Kiss
Tempting the Jaguar
Enemy Mine
Heart of the Jaguar

Moon Shifter Series
Alpha Instinct
Lover's Instinct
Primal Possession
Mating Instinct
His Untamed Desire
Avenger's Heat
Hunter Reborn
Protective Instinct
Dark Protector
A Mate for Christmas

Darkness Series
Darkness Awakened
Taste of Darkness
Beyond the Darkness
Hunted by Darkness
Into the Darkness
Saved by Darkness
Guardian of Darkness

Miami Scorcher Series
Unleashed Temptation
Worth the Risk
Power Unleashed
Dangerous Craving
Desire Unleashed

Crescent Moon Series
Taming the Alpha
Claiming His Mate
Tempting His Mate
Saving His Mate
To Catch His Mate
Falling For His Mate
Wolf's Mate

Futuristic Romance
Heated Mating
Claiming Her Warriors
Claimed by the Warrior

Contemporary Erotic Romance
Dangerous Deception
Everything to Lose
Adrianna's Cowboy
Tempting Alibi
Tempting Target
Tempting Trouble

ABOUT THE AUTHOR

Katie Reus is the *New York Times* and *USA Today* bestselling author of the Red Stone Security series, the Darkness series and the Redemption Harbor series. She fell in love with romance at a young age thanks to books she pilfered from her mom's stash. Years later she loves reading romance almost as much as she loves writing it.

However, she didn't always know she wanted to be a writer. After changing majors many times, she finally graduated summa cum laude with a degree in psychology. Not long after that she discovered a new love. Writing. She now spends her days writing dark paranormal romance and sexy romantic suspense.

For more information on Katie please visit her website: www.katiereus.com.